JUN 9. 93

MONS CRIMES UNIT

CONFIDENTIAL

FRANKENSTEIN'S MONSTER

LAPD

OCT 12. 84

RESTRICTED MATERIAL

DEC 11. 77

MAR 22. 04

D1625238

THE FRANKENSTEIN JOURNALS

GUTS or BUST

Written by Scott Sonneborn

Stone Arch Books
a Capstone Imprint

The Frankenstein Journals
is published by Stone Arch Books,
A Capstone Imprint
1710 Roe Crest Drive
North Mankato, Minnesota 56003
www.capstonepub.com

I dedicate this
journal to my dad.

Text copyright © 2016 Stone Arch Books
Illustrations copyright © Stone Arch Books

All rights reserved. No part of this publication may be reproduced in whole or in part, or stored in a retrieval system, or transmitted in any form or by any means, electronic, mechanical, photocopying, recording, or otherwise, without written permission of the publisher.

Cataloging-in-Publication Data is available on the Library of Congress website.
ISBN: 978-1-4965-0223-0 (paper over board)
ISBN: 978-1-4965-2361-7 (eBook)

Summary: Another day, another family member to find! JD is the fourteen-year-old son of Frankenstein's monster and is on a quest to find his family . . . the donors of his dad's mismatched parts. But with every cousin he meets, the danger mounts. New monsters lurk at every turn, and Fran will stop at nothing to get her hands on JD's cousins and enlists the help of the Werewolf and the Invisible Man! Readers will be pulled into the creepy story with tons of diary entries, mixed media images, artifacts, maps, and more as JD solves the secrets of his own rag-tag family!

Special thanks to Will, Ben, Ed, Dylan, Zach, and Ms. Prime's Class

Designer: Hilary Wacholz

Illustrated by Timothy Banks

Printed in China.
032015   008866RRDF15

No Guts, No Gloria

Chapter 1

Dear Future Me,

I hope everything's going great for you (meaning me) whenever you're reading this. Because right now, your (my) life has been nothing but crazy since I found Dr. Frankenstein's journal!

Yeah, if you forgot, there were two journals. Mine (this one) that I wrote everything down in so I would never forget everything that's happened.

I only had a few pages of Dr. Frankenstein's journal.

Like the ones where Frankenstein described where he found his monster's brain, eyeballs, and butt. I may not have had all the pages, but I definitely had the grossest ones! But while they did have a lot of disgusting junk in them, they didn't seem to have a ton of clues.

EEEK!

Clues I needed to save my family.

It was still weird to think that I had a big family out there . . . somewhere. Not that long ago I was living in Shelley's Orphanage for Lost and Neglected Children. Back then, I figured I didn't have any family at all. It wasn't until the orphanage went out of business that I found Dr. Frankenstein's journal.

I also found out that I was the son of Frankenstein's monster! I gotta admit — that did kind of freak me.

It also explained why one of my eyes was blue and the other green. Why one of my hands was way bigger than the other. And why my legs were two different sizes.

Body parts from dozens of people went into making my dad. And he had passed down all of their legs, feet, eyes, and hands to me.

All of those people whose parts went into my dad probably had relatives who were still alive. I was related to them too. They were like my cousins!

Cousins I had to find — and fast!

Because if I didn't, Fran Kenstein would get to them first. Fran was the daughter of Dr. Frankenstein, and she had stolen her dad's journal from me (luckily, I had copied a few of the pages first).

With the info she had from Dr. F's journal, Fran planned to use my cousins to build a new monster.

I didn't have anything against monsters. I mean, my dad was one. I had never met him, but I assumed he was a pretty nice guy.

But when I said that Fran planned to use my cousins, what I meant was that she planned to take a hand from one, a leg from another, and so on.

I couldn't let that happen to my family (even if I didn't know who they were). Which meant I had to warn my cousins before Fran could get to them.

But to warn them, I had to find them. That meant figuring out the clues in the pages I did have from Dr. Frankenstein's journal — like this one, about the Monster's large intestine.

Like I said, I may not have had all the pages, but I sure had the grossest ones. This one was full of disgusting pictures, but it didn't have much in the way of clues.

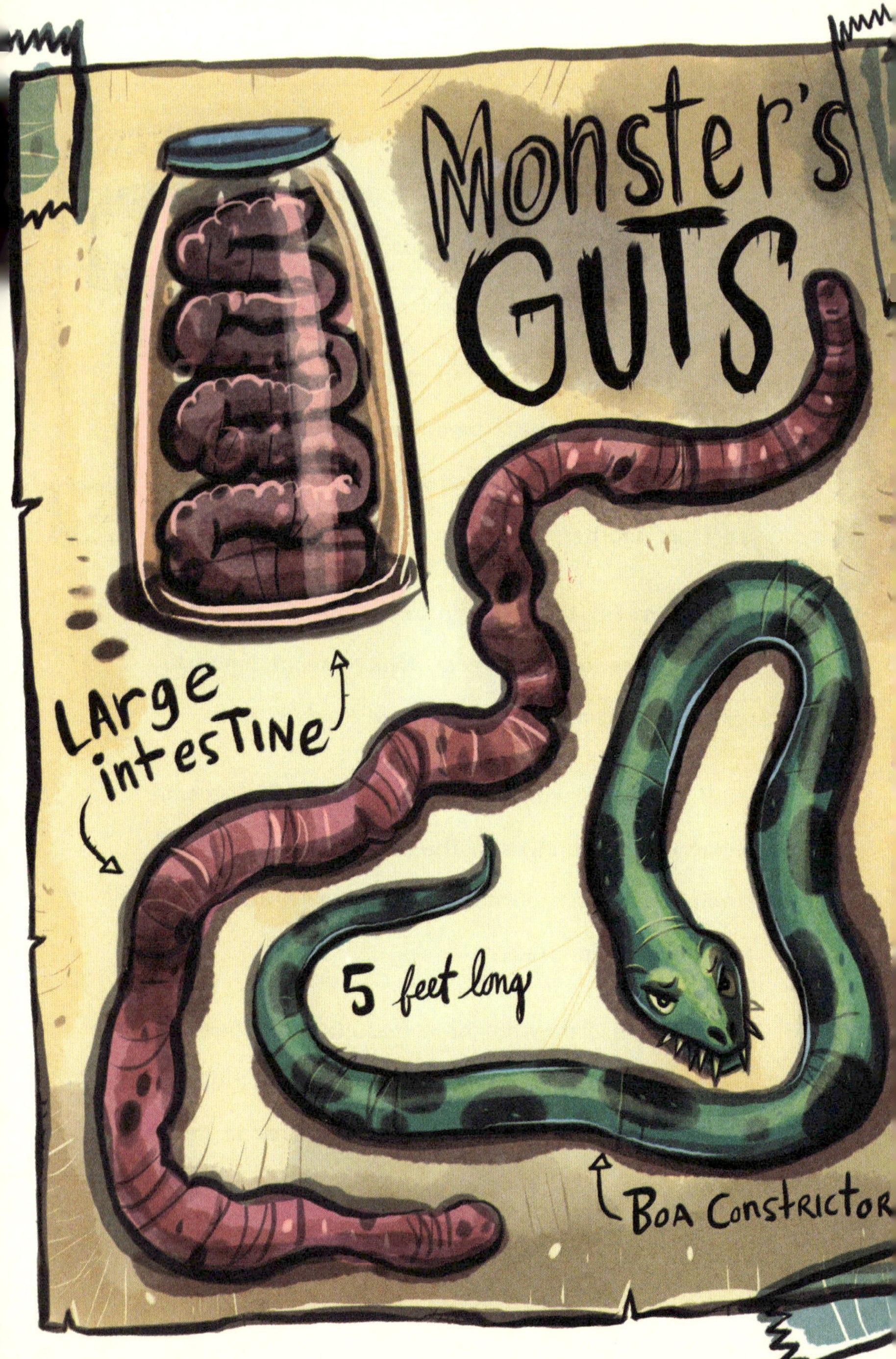

Monster's GUTS

LArge intesTine

5 feet long

BOA Constrictor

In fact, it only had a few words on it: "Large Intestine" and the "Monster's Guts." And since "guts" is just another word for large intestine, that didn't really tell me anything at all.

Of course, that wouldn't have stopped Sam.

Sam was my second cousin (the second cousin I had found, that is). His dad was a famous private eye whose actual eye had gone into my dad. Which is kind of gross, but also kind of cool. Because that's what made Sam related to me.

Sam was a police detective in Los Angeles. He'd know where to find clues in Dr. F's journal.

But Sam was still busy wrapping up the case I had helped him solve. Which I totally understood. (If you don't remember why it was so important that the guy we caught stay behind bars, just read the last part of my journal).

Sam didn't even have time to say goodbye. Instead, he gave me something:

My dad's police file from the Los Angeles Police Department Monster Crimes Unit!

I carried it around the corner from the LAPD headquarters, looking for a place to read it. I found a branch of the local library and sat down at a table.

I hoped my dad's file would help me solve the other big mystery in my life: what happened to him? Where did my dad go after he dropped me off at the orphanage and disappeared?

I may have had the eye of a detective, just like Sam, but I couldn't figure this mystery out.

I studied the police file backward and forward. There was some stuff about my dad from before I was born (no crimes, though. I guess he was a pretty good guy). But there was nothing in the file from after I was born.

Still, I hoped there might be some clue about where my dad might be. So my eyes lit up when I saw this:

When I saw that headline, I got excited.

Until I read the article. The monster in it wasn't my dad. It was the Vampire.

Sam once told me, "Just because a clue doesn't tell you everything, doesn't mean it's telling you nothing."

Maybe that was true. But this wasn't even a clue. It was just an old newspaper article that had been put in the wrong Monster Crimes Unit file.

Still, I knew Sam wouldn't just throw the article away. He'd look again to see if there was anything useful in it.

So I took another look. And that's when I saw it!

Under the photo, it said the Vampire's bodyguard had the nickname "The Monster's Guts" — because he was brave and he protected a monster.

I flipped back through the pages I had from Dr. Frankenstein's journal. On the page describing the large intestine, it also said the "Monster's Guts."

MONSTER IN MIAMI

The Vampire, pictured with his bodyguard, Gilford Ennis, Ennis's bravery in the Vampire's service has earned him the nickname "The Monster's Guts."

Maybe Dr. Frankenstein hadn't written that as another way of saying "my monster's large intestine." Maybe it was the nickname of the man the intestine had come from!

That had to be it! That meant the article wasn't misfiled. It had been put in there because my dad got his large intestine from a guy who was the Vampire's bodyguard!

I just might have found where my dad got his guts!

Even better, I figured there was a chance the bodyguard might still be alive. I didn't know much about science or medicine (or a lot of things, really). But I did know that everyone has a large AND a small intestine. You don't need both, right?

Even if my medical knowledge was off, I knew the Vampire was still alive. Or, not alive, but undead or whatever. If a guy like that had kicked the bucket, it would definitely make the news. But I didn't find anything more about the Vampire on the Internet.

Except his email!

So I sent him an email. And he wrote back!

I had a lead on another cousin! Maybe I really did have the eye of a detective.

And the guts of a professional bodyguard!

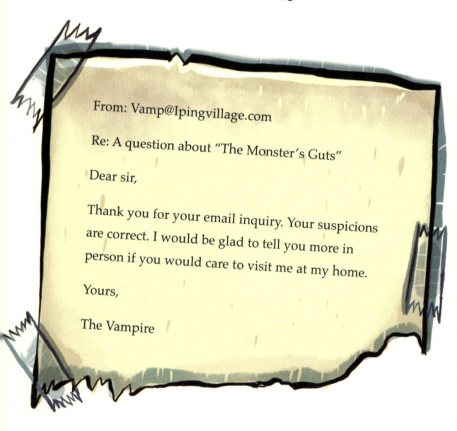

From: Vamp@Ipingvillage.com

Re: A question about "The Monster's Guts"

Dear sir,

Thank you for your email inquiry. Your suspicions are correct. I would be glad to tell you more in person if you would care to visit me at my home.

Yours,

The Vampire

Chapter 2

A day later, I was in Florida.

The Vampire's email had included a plane ticket. What it hadn't included were answers to any of my questions about his bodyguard. He just said we would talk when I met him at his home.

That turned out to be in a place called Iping Village. It was a retirement community near Miami, Florida.

The one security guard opened the front gate for me. "I bet you're here to see your grandparents," he said. "Go right in!"

I told him I was actually there to meet a cousin, who was related to me through my dad's large intestine.

The guard looked at me like I was crazy.

The Vampire had emailed me the address of his condo. So I started looking for it.

Iping Village was right by the beach, with lots of little houses on a golf course. Every few feet there was a kiosk, or key-ask, or whatever you call those stands that have posters and signs stuck on them.

All of them had signs advertising a show that was playing tonight:

The
IPING VILLAGE
COMMUNITY CENTER
presents
MIMES at 4PM
Get there at 3 for the EARLY BIRD DINNER

Who wants to see mimes? At four in the afternoon? Or eat dinner at three?

As I walked to the Vampire's condo, I saw the answer: old people.

Iping Village was full of them. Riding on golf carts. Slowly. Very slowly. Or walking — even more slowly — with four-pronged canes.

That's when I had a horrifying thought.

I had been wondering why the Vampire wanted to live in the sunniest place in the entire United States.

Suddenly, it all made sense. All these old people were easy pickings!

I mean, they couldn't move very fast (even on golf carts, their max speed was fifteen miles per hour).

Not to mention, in a place where the average age looked to be ninety years old, it was only natural that some people passed away every year.

If the Vampire got to a few of them early, who would notice?

Then I had an even more terrible thought: why did the Vampire invite me here instead of answering my questions over email? Was it because he was tired of only drinking old people and wanted some fresh blood?! ACK!

Despite the hot Florida sun, a shiver went down my spine. I didn't want to believe a cousin of mine would work for someone as evil as that.

But even if that made my cousin evil too, he didn't deserve what Fran Kenstein had in store for him. I had to warn him.

Without the Vampire getting his fangs in me!

YIKES!

The question was — how was I going to do that?

I had reached the door of the Vampire's condo. As I stood there trying to think, a dog lying outside started barking at me.

It was an old dog. It barely lifted its head to let out a . . .

Woof Woof!

"Hey there," I whispered. "Shhh! I'm trying to figure out how to warn my cousin who I'm related to through his large intestine without being sucked dry by the Vampire!"

It gave me the same look the security guard had. And kept barking.

I had to do something to quiet it down. I closed my eyes and tried to think of what to do.

Only to have someone rush up and tackle me to the ground!

Chapter 3

OOMPH! I hit the ground hard. Holding me down was a woman who was maybe twenty. Or thirty. It was hard to tell with her hand pushing my face down.

"Why are you lurking outside the Vampire's condo?" she asked.

"MRRRMPH," I replied. I was trying to say, "Please don't feed me to the Vampire!" But it was hard to talk with her hand on my mouth.

She took her hand off my mouth. "What do you want with the Vampire?" she asked.

"He invited me here! My name's JD! I just want to talk to him," I cried, "about his bodyguard."

As proof, I pointed to my journal, which had fallen out of my back pocket. The newspaper article about the Vampire's bodyguard was sticking out of it.

"I'm the Vampire's bodyguard," said the woman as she got off of me. The dog hadn't moved but continued to bark at me.

The woman took my journal and looked at the picture. I looked at it, too. And then at the woman who had tackled me.

"You're the Vampire's bodyguard? You look a little shorter now," I said. "And also more like a girl. And also can you get this dog to stop barking? And also . . . didn't the Vampire tell you I was coming?!"

As she studied the picture, she told the dog, "Good boy, Renfield. This is JD."

The dog stopped barking immediately.

"Renfield is the Vampire's dog," the woman explained. "He doesn't move much, but he's an excellent alarm dog. I trained him to bark at anyone he's never seen before. Now that he's met you, JD, he'll never bark at you again."

Then she turned to me. "And yes, the Vampire did say you were coming. But you're not what I was expecting. You have to admit, you do look a bit peculiar."

I nodded. When you have one blue eye and one green, and one hand a lot bigger than the other, you get that a lot.

"Well, anyway, I'm okay," I said, getting to my feet. "I guess it was just a mix-up. No need to apologize."

"You're right," she replied. "That's why I didn't apologize. A bodyguard has to assess every potential risk to her client and act accordingly. I acted accordingly."

She looked at the newspaper photograph of the Vampire and his bodyguard.

"That's my father in the picture," she said. "He was the Vampire's bodyguard. I've got the job now. My name's Gloria."

As she looked at her dad's face in the photo, her mouth turned very slightly in the corners. It took me a second to recognize what her mouth was doing. She was smiling. By the time I figured it out, the tiny smile was gone.

Instead, she was staring at me. Suspiciously.

"And since I'm his bodyguard now," she said coldly, "it's my job to ask: why are you curious about the Vampire's security?"

I told her my whole story, including how Fran Kenstein would be after her because she was my cousin.

I must have talked for ten minutes straight!

She listened carefully the whole time, concentrating on every word.

Finally, when I was done, she said, "Okay, got it."

That wasn't exactly the reaction I was expecting. I sort of thought she'd be surprised to hear about me, my dad, and Fran Kenstein.

It's not exactly your typical fourteen-year-old's life story.

Not to mention, a big part of that story was how her father's guts ended up in my dad!

"I'm sorry to have to tell you about that," I said. "I mean, it's not like it was my fault. Or my dad's fault. But still . . ."

"Don't apologize. You had to tell me that so I could adequately assess the risk Fran Kenstein poses. A bodyguard needs to know the risks to do her job," Gloria said.

"I am not happy to hear about what happened to my father after he died," she said in a tone of voice that didn't sound sad. Or happy. It was all business. "But I don't have time to be sad right now. I have a job to do. The same job my family has always done: keep the Vampire safe while he sleeps during the day like he's doing now."

"That's your family's job?" I asked, confused.

"Protecting the Vampire has always been my family's responsibility," Gloria explained. "In fact, only someone in my family can do it."

"I don't understand," I said.

"Most people don't," she said, handing me a business card. "But a bodyguard doesn't have time to stand around answering everyone's questions about the rules the Vampire lives by. So I made this."

The top of the card read "Vampire FAQ." Below that were all sorts of questions and answers about the Vampire:

Vampire FAQ
(FRequently Annoying Questions)

- Can the Vampire enter a house without being invited?

  Unless it's your own home, entering a house without being invited is breaking and entering. No one can do that under federal law. That includes the Vampire.

- When can the Vampire go outside?

  The Vampire can <u>ONLY</u> go out at night. He will explode if he goes out in the sun.

- So can he go outside on a cloudy day?

  No.

- How about a rainy, cloudy day?

  No!

- How about a day that's —

  NO! He can <u>ONLY</u> go out after sundown.

- Why is your family the only ones who can look after the Vampire?

  The Vampire can only make a pact with one family to be his bodyguard. No one else can protect him.

- Yeah, but why is that?

  Because that's the <u>RULE.</u>

- But what would happen if someone else tries to protect him?

  I don't even want to know the answer to that. So, trust me — if I don't want to know, you don't want to know.

"No one else can protect the Vampire while he sleeps but a member of my family," said Gloria. "My grandfather protected the Vampire. When my grandfather died, my dad became the Vampire's bodyguard.

"When he died, it became my job," said Gloria. "And it's a dangerous job — the Vampire has made a few enemies in the past four hundred years. One in particular."

Gloria looked around.

"Who are you looking for?" I asked.

"No one," she replied. "You can't look for someone you can't see."

I had no idea what that meant. But before I could ask, she turned and looked into my eye (the green one).

"You came here to warn me about the threat posed to my person by Ms. Kenstein," she said. "And you've done that. So please go. I can't afford any distractions while I'm on duty."

She was too busy looking around to even look at me when she said the words.

I didn't know what to say either. Every other cousin I had found had been happy to meet me.

But I guess I had to expect that not all of them would be like that. Still, I had only found three relatives so far. The fact that one wanted me to get lost was pretty disappointing.

Okay, more than disappointing. But whatever. I had a lot more cousins to find and warn about Fran. I had already told Gloria everything she needed to know. Besides, she seemed like she could take care of herself. It wasn't like she needed my help. She had definitely made that clear.

So I said goodbye and headed off to find more cousins who actually wanted me around.

On my way out of Iping Village, I walked across the golf course.

There was one of those kiosks or whatever they're called with a poster for the mime show. It was kind of shady underneath it. Renfield had found his way there (I guess he could move, just really slowly) and was resting in a cool spot.

There was no one else around. It seemed like all the other old people here were kind of like the Vampire and liked to take a long nap during the day.

So I sat there next to Renfield to write down what had happened in my journal.

But as soon as I started, Renfield barked. And barked. It couldn't have been because of me. Gloria had said that Renfield was trained to bark at people he hadn't seen before. But he had already met me.

So I looked up from my journal to find out why Renfield was barking. And saw . . .

Chapter 4

I stared at Fran Kenstein across the eighth hole of the Iping Village golf course.

How could she be here?! She didn't have my dad's police file, and that's what had led me to Gloria.

Apparently, she had the same question for me.

"How are you here?!" asked Fran. "How could you have found out about Gloria before me — when only I have access to all of Dr. Frankenstein's journal?"

That was true. Fran did have all the pages of her father's journal.

But only because she had stolen them from me!

"I guess I shouldn't be surprised," said Fran. "You've already inconvenienced me twice. I thought that framing you and having you arrested would get you out of the way. Apparently not."

She smiled. Which freaked me out. Anything that made Fran happy was not good news for me.

"So I went back to my lab and invented this!" she exclaimed as she pulled out a hair dryer.

"I think someone else already invented the hair dryer," I told her.

"I know that!" she shouted. "I'm a lot smarter than you, after all! Which is why no one else could have transformed an ordinary hair dryer into an AIR FRYER!"

"Um, I think someone invented that too. Isn't an air fryer a thing you can use to cook French fries and fried chicken?" I asked.

Fran turned red.

"Okay, so maybe I need to think of a better name," she admitted. "This Air Fryer doesn't make chicken. It can light air on fire!"

And then she pointed it at me.

"And since you are surrounded by air, that's not good for you." Fran laughed. "It's funny, really — using what used to be a hair dryer to get you out of my hair. Forever!"

I didn't think that was funny at all. I actually found it pretty terrifying. I was so scared, the only part of me I could get to move was my eyelids. I slammed them shut so I wouldn't have to see what was about to happen to me. But I could still hear as Fran shouted, "Goodbye, ughmmmgh!!"

Huh. That wasn't exactly what I expected her last words to me to be.

I risked opening an eye (the green one) and saw Fran on the ground — with Gloria on top of her. She had tackled Fran just like she had tackled me!

Renfield's barking must have brought Gloria running. And just in time! I was safe.

But Gloria wasn't.

"Thank you for saving me the trouble of finding you. You're the one I'm here for," said Fran as her hand reached toward the Air Fryer, which had fallen to the ground.

"Look out, Gloria!" I cried.

Gloria looked confused: "Why? What's she going to do with a hair dry —"

Before I could do anything else, Fran fired! Suddenly, the air burst into flames!

WOOOOOOSH!

Chapter 5

Luckily, Gloria was looking at the Air Fryer when Fran pulled the trigger.

Gloria rolled out of the way just as the air around her caught fire!

The blaze only lasted a second. But that was long enough to melt the bottom of the kiosk advertising tonight's mime show. The heavy kiosk fell over — right on Gloria's legs!

She was hurt. Bad. It didn't look like she could move her legs.

But that didn't stop her from grabbing the Air Fryer out of Fran's hands and aiming it right back at her!

Fran scrambled to her feet and backed away.

"Don't shoot! I'm going!" she cried. She backed away. "After all, I've got plenty more people to visit. Don't I, JD? You won't be able to get to all of them first!"

As Fran ran off, Gloria tried to get up to chase after her. But Gloria couldn't even get to her feet. She stumbled back to the ground.

That's when I realized I had been standing in the same spot the whole time. I hadn't moved at all!

I raced over to Gloria.

"Are you okay?" I asked. "Are you bleeding?"

"I don't have time to bleed," she replied, as she tried to get to her feet again. "I've got a job to do."

It took all the guts I had to look at her legs.

I don't like blood. So it was lucky for both of us that her legs weren't bleeding. But she couldn't stand.

"This is what happens when a bodyguard doesn't assess risks properly," she said as she looked at the Air Fryer in her hands. "I thought this was just a hair dryer. Now I'm too injured to walk."

"I'm sorry," I told her. "This wouldn't have happened if you hadn't saved me."

"Yes, that was another mistake no bodyguard should make," Gloria nodded sadly. "Leaving her client when danger is present."

"Then why'd you do it?" I asked, pretty upset that she had called saving my life a mistake.

"Do you really have to ask, JD?" she said, looking more hurt than when the kiosk fell on her legs.

"Well, yeah," I replied. "I mean, you seemed pretty eager to get rid of me. You said I was just a distraction!"

"I did say you were a distraction," said Gloria. "And I meant it. Being a good bodyguard is very important to me, JD. Because it's what my family does. I care about my job because I care about my family."

She looked at me and added, "And you're family, JD."

"When a bodyguard is on duty," she said, "all she's supposed to care about is her client. Having someone like you around that I care about is a distraction."

"Oh," was all I could think to say.

"Now I have to get back to work," she said, all business again. "Get me over to a golf cart."

There was one sitting nearby next to the golf course. I helped Gloria toward the driver's seat.

"The other side," she told me. "You're going to have to drive. My legs can't work the pedals."

I did what she said and got behind the wheel. It was the first time I had driven anything. Which would have been cool, if it weren't for Gloria.

"Which way to the hospital?" I asked as we drove off.

"No hospital," replied Gloria. "Someone still has to protect the Vampire. Drive me back to his condo — and fast."

I did what she asked, but I didn't like it. Gloria wasn't bleeding or anything, but her legs probably needed casts or bandages or something.

"Can't the Vampire take care of himself?" I asked her. "I mean, he's the Vampire!"

"He is the Vampire," agreed Gloria as we rode on the golf cart. "But think about it. He's four hundred years old. That's old. And like most really old people, he sleeps all day. Sure, in a coffin instead of on the couch. But still. He can't even go outside when the sun is up. Twelve hours out of every day, he's totally vulnerable unless I'm there to protect him."

"If he's so allergic to the sun, why is he living here in Miami, Florida?" I asked. "It doesn't get much sunnier than this!"

"I agree," said Gloria. "I told him he'd be much safer in Alaska or Antarctica or somewhere else that doesn't get much sun. But he wanted to be here, because he likes to be around older people."

Oh man! So I had been right!

"You mean because they won't put up a fight when he sucks their blood!" I exclaimed. "And because no one will be surprised if a ninety-year-old dies in the middle of the night!"

"What? No!" said Gloria. "You have some imagination! The Vampire has been a vegetarian for years."

GROSS!

Huh?! So much for my theory. "But if the Vampire doesn't want to bite them, why does he like old people so much?" I asked.

"The Vampire has lived for a long time," Gloria explained as we crossed the last hole of the golf course. "And like most people who have lived a long time, his favorite memories are from when he was younger. The old people who live here are the only ones who know about the things from the 1940s and 1950s that the Vampire likes to remember. Like Frank Sinatra. And black-and-white movies."

"And mimes," I added, pointing at a poster of the night's mime show as we drove past it.

"Right," she nodded. "I've never seen a mime show. Have you?"

I shook my head no.

"No one under eighty has. That's why the Vampire lives here," said Gloria. "And while I think the sun is an unnecessary risk, there are some things I do like about this place. For one, older people tend to eat very bland food. You won't find any garlic around here. That takes one risk factor out of play. And as a bodyguard, I've got to look out for every risk."

"You make the Vampire sound like a nice guy," I said. "So why does he need a bodyguard?"

"Four hundred years is a long time to live. Even the nicest person is going to make mistakes and rub some people the wrong way," she said. "Or in the Vampire's case, one person."

As she said that, Gloria looked around.

"Who?" I asked. "Who are you looking for?"

"Nobody," she replied. "You can't look out for someone you can't see."

"What do you mean?" I asked.

But Gloria wasn't listening. We were driving past the Iping Village Community Theater.

Gloria was looking at a group of men dressed all in black with white painted faces. The mimes had arrived for their show tonight.

Gloria stared at one of the mimes. Most were tall and skinny. This one was short and fat.

"It's him," whispered Gloria. "He's here!"

Suddenly, the fat mime wiped off his face paint. Underneath wasn't a face. In fact, there wasn't anything there at all!

Even weirder, he started taking off all his clothes!

There was nothing under them either!

I didn't understand what I was seeing (or not seeing).

Gloria did.

"That's the Vampire's archenemy," she told me. "That's the Invisible Man."

Chapter 6

"Drive faster!" cried Gloria. "We've got to get to the Vampire's condo before he does!"

I pushed my foot down as far as it would go, and we raced off.

Well, "raced off" is kind of an exaggeration. I made the golf cart go as fast as it could, but I probably could have run faster.

But Gloria couldn't.

"What's happening?" I asked her. "How did that mime just disappear?"

"That was no mime," said Gloria. "That was the Invisible Man. Remember when I said there was one person the Vampire had rubbed the wrong way? It was the Invisible Man. He must have disguised himself as a mime to get in here with them."

I had never seen anything about the Invisible Man on the Internet. But I guess that kind of made sense. I mean, it's hard to see a lot about someone you can't see.

"He's been trying to get revenge on the Vampire for years," said Gloria. "My family has always stopped him."

"What did the Vampire do to him?" I asked.

Gloria wasn't sure exactly. It had something to do with the Invisible Woman. But whatever it was happened years ago. The Vampire hadn't seen the Invisible Woman in a long time.

"Well, he never actually SAW her," said Gloria. "She is invisible. But, they were dating behind the Invisible Man's back. Or maybe in front of his back too. It's kind of hard to tell with invisible people."

"That sounds kind of complicated," I said.

"Not for me," Gloria replied. "When you're a bodyguard, everything is simple. It all comes down to doing whatever it takes to keep your client safe."

We pulled up in front of the Vampire's condo. I helped Gloria inside.

In the living room, where the couch should have been, was a coffin. A huge coffin. It looked like it weighed a ton (or maybe ten tons? How much is a ton? Anyway, it must have weighed a lot).

"Whoa!" I said. "Is the Vampire . . ."

"Yes," replied Gloria as she went to the coffin. "The Vampire is safe in there. For now. The coffin can only be opened from the inside. Unless you have this."

She pressed the side of the coffin. A panel popped
open. Gloria took out the key that was hidden inside.

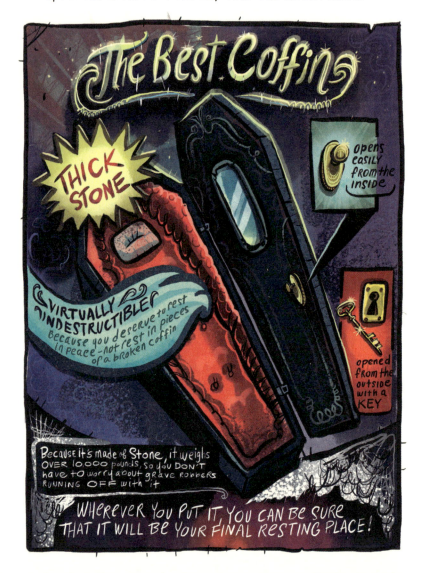

"The coffin is indestructible," she explained to me carefully. "The Invisible Man knows he won't be able to get inside and get his revenge unless he has this key."

"So why'd you just take the key out of its hiding place?" I asked.

"The Invisible Man knows all about the key and the coffin," she replied. "He and the Vampire used to be good friends, remember?"

"Okay, so let's use that key and get the Vampire out of here!" I said.

Gloria looked out through the window. "There's still some time until sundown," she said. "Taking him out of his coffin now would destroy him."

One thing was for sure — we weren't going to move the Vampire inside the coffin. Whatever made it indestructible also made it incredibly heavy.

OUCH!

"I can't fight the Invisible Man," said Gloria as she took some bandages from the Vampire's bathroom and wrapped up her legs. "And I won't be quick enough to keep the key away from him either."

"Don't panic," I told her. "I'll figure something out."

That's what I always said when I found myself in trouble. Sometimes, I said it to pump myself up without totally believing it.

This time, I didn't believe it at all. But Gloria seemed to. She wasn't panicking at all.

"That's correct. You are going to have to figure it out, JD," she said. "Because you're the only one who can."

Gloria held up the key.

"According to the Vampire's rules, only a member of my family can protect him," she said.

I started to ask "why," but Gloria held up her card. The one with the "Frequently Annoying Questions."

"I don't have time to explain the Vampire's rules on a normal day," she said. "And this is not a normal day. You're the only one who can do this. But I promised to protect the Vampire. It's what our family has always done."

I was part of that family. I was the only one who could help her. There was just one problem.

"I don't know how to be a bodyguard!" I said.

"All it takes," Gloria told me, "is everything. You have to be willing to do everything you can to make sure nothing happens to the person you're protecting."

She turned and looked me in the eye (the blue one this time). "The only question is," she said, "do you have enough guts?"

I knew the answer immediately. Of course, I didn't have the guts!

Chapter 7

I was scared out of my mind. How could Gloria and I be related? Nothing scared her! She had way more guts than I did!

But then I remembered that the guts she had were inherited from her dad. Which meant they were in me too — because they had been in my dad.

She was family. And now that I'd found her, I didn't want to lose her. Which maybe I would, if she tried to protect the Vampire on her own without being able to use her legs.

"Give me the key," I told her. "If you think I can keep it away from that invisible guy, I'll try my best."

"I never said I thought you could keep it away from him," said Gloria, handing me the key. "I believe the risk is lower with you. I estimate that giving you the key reduces the risk to my client by twenty percent."

"Whoa — wait!" I exclaimed. "So you're saying I've only got a twenty percent chance of getting out of here without some crazed guy I can't even see grabbing me!?!?"

WHAT????

"No," replied Gloria calmly. "I estimate my odds of evading the Invisible Man with two injured legs are approximately five percent. Giving you the key increases my client's odds by twenty percent. In other words, you have a six percent chance of success."

"Oh," was all I could think to say — before a crashing sound made both of us turn our heads toward the door.

BOOM!!!

"The Invisible Man is coming," said Gloria evenly. "Your odds are dropping by the second. I suggest you go. Now."

The door swung open like it had been kicked in. But no one was there.

Gloria moved to block the door — only to fly off her feet. She hung there, a yard off the ground.

"Where is the key?" demanded the Invisible Man. "Tell me quick. I grow tired of holding you aloft."

"Put her down!" I shouted. "I have it!"

"JD, don't," said Gloria, raising her voice for the first time. "This isn't about me!"

It was for me. But I didn't stand around to argue with her. I took off running. And hoped the Invisible Man followed.

I looked over my shoulder and saw Gloria fall to the ground. She was okay.

But somewhere between me and her was the Invisible Man.

I was glad I had gotten him to leave Gloria without hurting her.

Now I just had to make sure he didn't hurt me!

I raced to a window, pushed it open, and jumped outside.

I hit the ground and started running.

I had two choices: find a way to fight the Invisible Man or find a place to hide.

I guess that might have been a tough decision for some people.

For me, it was easy. Of course I was going to hide!

I made a loop around the Vampire's condo and opened the door to the nearest building.

It was the small community library with books and board games. Inside, it was dark and empty.

I closed the door quietly behind me, then risked a peek out the window.

I didn't see anything. Nothing at all.

Not even the Invisible Man's face, which was right there staring back at me!

Chapter 8

Of course, I only realized that when — CRASH! — the window smashed in on me.

I could feel a hand grabbing at me. But I couldn't see it. I could only smell the hint of sweat as the Invisible Man struggled to reach me.

I backed away from the broken window.

"I grow weary of this chase," wheezed the Invisible Man, slightly out of breath. "Give me the key."

Suddenly, a couch floated up and came flying at me. And then a table and a chair.

I dodged the first two. But the chair hit me and bruised my arm numb.

That's when something else hit me too: the furniture wasn't flying on its own. The Invisible Man was throwing it!

Another chair (a really big one) levitated into the air. But instead of flying at me, it was smashed to pieces.

The message was clear. If the Invisible Man got his hands on me, the same thing would happen to me!

I crept back into the shadows of the darkened library and tried to hide behind a shelf of books.

I was definitely proving how much guts I had.

None.

Then suddenly, I heard a . . .

CREEEEEEEAK.

It was the bookshelf I was hiding behind. The Invisible Man was right there on the other side, trying to topple it on me!

"**URRH!**" he groaned as he shoved. He was so close that I could smell his sweat as he pushed hard.

The shelf was so overloaded with books, it took him maybe three seconds of pushing to get it to fall over. Which was just enough time for me to scramble out of the way, as **WHOOMP!** it crashed to the floor.

The Invisible Man had to climb over the fallen shelf, giving me time to run out of the library.

I had to find somewhere else to hide. If he could get that close without me knowing, there's no way I'd escape if he found me again.

Outside, I ran past Renfield, sleeping on the grass.

He lifted his head an inch above the ground and let out a loud **WOOOOOF!**

"Shh!" I pleaded. "I need to hide. I know it's not what Gloria would do, but I'm kind of new at trying to be brave and —"

I stopped trying to justify myself to a dog when I realized Renfield wasn't barking at me. Only there wasn't anyone else around. Renfield must have been barking at the Invisible Man!

Gloria had said she'd trained Renfield to bark at anyone he hadn't seen before. Well, there was no way Renfield had ever seen the Invisible Man!

But Renfield could smell him. I took off in the opposite direction, silently reminding myself to thank the old dog, if (I meant "when" — stay positive!) I survived all this.

And I really did need to thank him. Not only had Renfield's bark warned me the Invisible Man was close (it sure would have been great if Renfield could move fast enough to stay with me as I ran) — he had also given me an idea.

Renfield had smelled the Invisible Man. I had, too, when he was close enough to grab me. He was certainly working up quite a sweat chasing after me.

I remembered that when he was dressed as a mime, he kind of stood out as being overweight. Which I guess made sense: if you're invisible, you don't have any motivation to go to the gym to try to look good.

If he were out of shape, then the more I could make him run, the sweatier he would get. Maybe I could get him so sweaty, I could smell his BO coming. I could use my nose instead of my eyes!

I wasn't sure that was a great plan.

In fact, I hoped it really stank!

Chapter 9

I ran for a long time.

That's really all there is to say.

I ran and thought about what the Invisible Man
had done to that chair — and hoped he didn't get the
chance to do that to me.

*　*　*

I must have run for hours. I ran past the theater,
all over the golf course, and around the condos. I
don't know how many laps I made of Iping Village.

IIPING VILLAGE

I kind of lost track of time. It was actually kind
of boring. Or would have been if I wasn't completely
scared out of my mind.

Of course, it would have been easier if I could have just run out of Iping Village and gone somewhere (anywhere) else.

But one whole side of the place ended at the beach. I guess I could have tried to swim for it. But I was staying ahead of the Invisible Man by running. I didn't know if he'd be faster than me in the water.

The rest of Iping Village was surrounded by a huge fence. There was only one gate. I ran by it a bunch of times, but the security guard had it closed. I never had time to stop and explain why he should open it for me, because the Invisible Man was right behind me.

PEWW!

I knew that because my plan was working. I could smell his BO a mile away.

Okay, maybe not a mile. But far enough that I had time to run in a different direction when I smelled him coming too close.

As long as I could keep this up, I could keep the key away from him.

There were just a couple problems with doing that. One: it was kind of embarrassing.

None of the old folks were outside to see me. I guessed they were all still taking their afternoon naps, just like the Vampire.

The only people outside were the mimes, who were holding up the clothes the Invisible Man had been disguised in. They seemed totally surprised that one of them had just disappeared and were trying to tell the security guard what happened.

Well, they weren't exactly trying to tell him. I guess they took their miming — or whatever you call it — very seriously. They didn't say a word. They just flapped their arms and waved their hands.

I guess I can't really blame the guard for looking at them like they were crazy. I must have looked even crazier to him every time I ran past him as I made my loop of Iping Village. I was running for my life, but he couldn't tell anyone was chasing me.

So I'm sure I looked like a crazy person.

I mean, I am literally sure. Because each time I ran past him, the guard yelled, "What are you doing!?! Are you crazy!?"

Like I said, I didn't have time to explain that I wasn't crazy (not that he would have believed me) because the Invisible Man was right behind.

And anyway, I could handle a little embarrassment.

What I couldn't handle was all the running. One of my legs was shorter than the other, and both of my feet were super huge. That made running hard.

I was getting tired. Really tired. Pretty soon, I'd have to stop.

Which, on the one hand, would be good. At least I'd stop embarrassing myself in front of the guard.

On the other hand, the Invisible Man would catch me, get the key, and do who knows what to the Vampire.

Not to mention me.

I ran out of steam as I was passing the security guard for the nineteenth time.

My legs just wouldn't run anymore. I pitched forward and collapsed.

Right onto the golf cart next to the security guard!

I hopped in and drove off!

"What're you doing?! Are you crazy?" cried the guard again. "That's my cart. Stop!"

The mimes all stuck out their palms at me, echoing his calls to stop.

But I didn't listen. (Can you "listen" to people who aren't talking? That sounded like a question I should ask the guy I couldn't see. Which I would have if he weren't trying to smash me.)

The security guard hopped onto another golf cart and chased after me.

As he pulled up alongside, I finally had the chance to explain to him how I was being chased by the Invisible Man who wanted the key to the Vampire's coffin that I had gotten from my cousin who was related to me through my dad's large intestine.

Even as I said it, I knew it made no sense.

The guard seemed to agree. "You really are crazy!" he said.

And then he flew out of his golf cart and landed on the ground.

"Hey, who did that?" said the guard as he stumbled to his feet.

I already knew the answer — the Invisible Man.

He got behind the wheel of the guard's golf cart and chased after me. Slowly. Very slowly.

I could have gotten out and run faster than we were driving.

But I was too tired to run.

Luckily, so was the Invisible Man.

I could hear him wheezing in his cart. He was too busy catching his breath to say anything as he chased me across Iping Village.

And then suddenly I stopped.

VRRRRRR! My golf cart's wheels kicked up sand. I had taken a wrong turn and gotten stuck on the beach!

Having run all over Iping nineteen times, I guess I should have known the place better. But it was starting to get dark and I was too busy being scared out of my mind to really watch where I was going.

The Invisible Man followed me onto the beach and got his cart stuck too. But that didn't stop him. I could see his footprints coming toward me in the sand.

Hey, wait! I could see his footprints in the sand!

I hopped off my cart and ran across the beach. I had gotten a bit of rest while driving the golf cart. Enough to run a little more.

And I knew where to run because I could see the Invisible Man's footprints under the now-setting sun. So I knew where he was!

Unfortunately, it wasn't long before the Invisible Man figured that out. He ran straight into the surf (I guess he had caught his breath too).

The waves were breaking hard. I couldn't tell where he was in the water.

Even worse — the ocean water was like a bath. Now I couldn't smell him either!

And even even worse — the sun was going down. It was getting darker.

And even even even worse — well, no. That was as bad as it got. But that was bad enough!

The Invisible Man could have been anywhere. I couldn't smell him. I couldn't see him. It was so dark I couldn't see anything.

Until the air lit up on fire!

"JD! Over here!" said Gloria. She was in another cart at the edge of the sand. She fired another burst from the Air Fryer that lit up the beach.

I saw footprints in the sand. The Invisible Man was coming for me.

And then, just as the flames from the Air Fryer died away, I saw something else.

Next to Gloria, there was someone behind the wheel of the cart. In the dim moonlight, it was too hard for me to see who it was.

Until he rushed right past me, and I saw . . .

The Vampire!

"No," cried the Invisible Man. "I was going to have my revenge!"

"Yes, you vere," said the Vampire, in whatever kind of weird accent the Vampire had. "But dees boy made you vait too long. It ees now night. Too late vor you!"

I really couldn't see what happened next. Between the Vampire's black cape and the Invisible Man being invisible, I couldn't tell what the two were doing in the darkening night.

I heard a "Hrnnn!" and then a "Ommph!" and then "**SCRREEECH!**" and then a "**SHOOPH!**" that might have been a hiss of smoke. And then the Vampire and the Invisible Man were gone!

COOL!

Chapter 10

The next morning, I woke up in the Vampire's condo.

No, not in his casket.

Gloria had invited me to sleep on the couch. As I
slid off it, both my legs burned from all the running
I had done the day before. But I couldn't complain
about my legs. Gloria had new casts on both of hers.

It would take a little time for them to get better,
but that was okay. She had time.

Whatever had happened to the Invisible Man (Gloria
wouldn't tell me), he wouldn't be back for a while.

In the meantime, she could get around Iping Village on a golf cart.

I offered to stay and help her, but she told me no. I understood. "I guess I showed yesterday how much help I would be to a bodyguard," I said. "I mean, when things got scary, all I could think to do was run or hide!"

"That's right, JD," she replied. "You did show how much help you could be last night. And all you did was . . . save my client!

"What you did last night was the bravest thing I've ever seen," she said. "I told you that you only had a six percent chance of success, and you agreed to help anyway. Being brave doesn't mean you're never scared. It means that even when things are scary, you still agree to take on the jobs that need to get done."

"You're exactly the kind of person whose help I could use, JD," she said.

"Oh," was all I could think to say. "Thank you."

"You shouldn't be so surprised," said Gloria. "We both got our guts from my father. He was the bravest man I ever knew.

"But I can't let you stay, JD," she went on. "Because you've got another scary job that needs doing. You've got to warn the rest of your cousins about Fran. Now that I know what she looks like, her risk to me is somewhere between low and minimal. Your other cousins are at a much higher risk, if you don't get to them first."

She handed me a bag. After I had fallen asleep on the couch, the Vampire had returned. He had taken the key from my pocket, but before he got back in his casket (I guess he was in there right now!), he had left the bag with Gloria to give to me.

"He wanted to give you a little something to thank you for helping keep him safe," she said.

The bag may have been little, but it sure was something. Inside were a handful of gold coins!

"Whoa," I said. "These look old. Are they from the last century?"

"Try three centuries before that," she told me. "They should be worth enough to get you wherever you need to go to find your next dozen cousins."

Tracking down my first three cousins hadn't been easy. Thinking about what it would take to find the next twelve filled me with a gust of fear. It sure would have been easier with Gloria's help. But she had a job to do.

So did I. And with the gold coins in one back pocket and my journal in the other, I headed out to do it!

NEXT...

RRRRRRRT!

A Pain in the Butt

Chapter 11

Hey, so, hello, my future self!

Since you've probably already read the previous chapters in my journal, you should know the drill: I wrote all this stuff down in my journal so you would always remember the story of how I met all my cousins.

I guess there's a chance parts of my journal might have been lost. Or stolen. Or maybe your mind got wiped fighting in the robot wars or whatever it is people are doing thirty years from now.

In that case, here's what you need to know:

My name is JD. I grew up in an orphanage. No one knew who had left me. So Mr. Shelley, the orphanage director, named me John Doe.

JD for short.

Growing up in the orphanage, the one thing I wanted was a big family. And then one day I found Dr. Victor Von Frankenstein's journal. In it, he revealed all the secrets about how he created his monster.

The journal also held an even bigger secret (at least to me). I was the son of . . .

FRANKENSTEIN'S MONSTER!

I've got to admit it was a shock to find out I was the son of a famous monster. Mostly because it meant I had a HUGE family!

Think about it. I inherited all my mismatched arms and hands and ears from my dad.

The way I figured it, the people he got those body parts from were my relatives. I have their legs, feet, and eyes, the same way other kids have their grandmother's ears or their great-uncle's nose.

Of course, those people were probably all dead. (At least, I hoped they were dead before Dr. Frankenstein took parts from their bodies and put them in my dad!)

But those people probably had kids and grandkids. They would be related to me too — they'd be like my cousins!

All I had to do was find out who they were. The clues I needed were all in Dr. Frankenstein's journal. And since I already mentioned that I had found Dr. F's journal, that should have been a piece of cake, right?

Wrong.

Dr. Frankenstein's daughter Fran Kenstein stole the journal from me. The only thing I had now were copies of just a few of the pages.

Fran also wanted to find my cousins — to use them to make a new monster.

And by "use them," I mean chop them up and take their body parts! So I had to find them first.

I had already found three: Robert, Sam, and Gloria.

Gloria was the Vampire's bodyguard. That's a job that took a ton of guts.

I had the same sort of guts Gloria did. That's how we were related: through my dad's large intestine.

That didn't mean I was as brave as Gloria, but I did my best when we ran into the Invisible Man and — well, that's a whole other story (Literally! Check out other parts of my journal, if you don't remember).

All you need to know now is that I helped Gloria protect the Vampire from the Invisible Man.

The Vampire was grateful. He was also immortal. That meant he'd kind of lived forever.

You know how old people tend to collect a lot of stuff over the years? Well, this guy was hundreds of years old. He had a ton of old stuff.

WOOOOO!

Including a bunch of gold coins.

He gave me a few to say "thank you."

Gloria still had her job to do, protecting the Vampire while he slept through the days in his retirement condo in Florida.

But with the gold coins he had given me, I had more than enough money to go anywhere in the world to meet the rest of my cousins.

Now I just had to figure out where to go.

Before Fran did!

DUN DUN DUN . . .

Chapter 12

I knew the clues I needed to find all of my cousins were in the pages of Dr. Frankenstein's journal.

Unfortunately, I didn't have all the pages. And the ones I had were all jumbled up and out of order.

What I needed was someone who could help me figure them out. Someone who knew all about Dr. Frankenstein and would be able to help me fill in what I was missing.

Of course, I had already met someone like that: Fran.

But there was no way she was helping me.

So I searched the Internet for other people who knew about Dr. F and his monster. And I found some. Most of them worked at the Department of Monster Studies at the Main Branch of the New York Public Library in Manhattan.

I had plenty of money, so that's where I went.

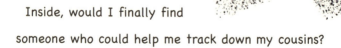

As I walked past the stone lions that guarded the library steps, I was nervous. Up until now, I had needed to figure out everything on my own.

Inside, would I finally find someone who could help me track down my cousins?

And maybe even my dad?

NOPE.

Turned out, due to budget cuts, the Department of Monster Studies was only open from noon until four. On Tuesdays. It was Wednesday. I was on my own again (at least until next Tuesday).

I found an empty table and took out my journal.

I spread out all the pages I had from Dr. F's journal.

I didn't have all of Dr. F's journal. That made it tough to figure what was written on the pages I did have.

What made it even tougher was that the pages seemed to be out of order.

Like, the one taped on the next page. It said "The End," but it was in the middle of the pages I had.

The End.

Another page said "Thanks to Princeton University," which I thought was maybe because Dr. F went there or something. You know, like he was thanking them for teaching him all the things he wrote about doing in his journal.

But as I spread all the pages I had from his journal out on the big wooden table, I saw something else.

Underneath "The End" there was a stain. Maybe it was from Dr. Frankenstein's coffee? Or lunch?

That didn't matter. What did matter was that it was only half a stain. Like half of the lunch (or coffee) had fallen on this page and half on another page.

I rifled through the pages I had. And then I found it! The stains matched! "The End" didn't mean the end of the book. It meant the end, as in REAR END.

In other words, the butt!   HAHAHAHA!

I had a clue!

Acquired 8:07 pm, Sept. 26
width 24"
18"
height
TOP SECRET
50 lbs
weight

Frankenstein hadn't written "Thanks to Princeton University" to say thank you for his education.

Somehow, Dr. F had gotten my dad's butt thanks to Princeton University.

I ran to the library's computer room and typed in "Princeton" and "Rear End." I got a stern warning from the librarian because the library has strict rules about using their computers for naughty pictures!

Once I convinced her that wasn't what I was doing, I found what I was looking for.

Bertram Wodehouse III.

He had gone to Princeton. As had his father and grandfather. Like them, Bertram III had donated a lot of money to the university when he died.

Unlike them, he had also donated his body! His body was given to the biology department so they could use it for "the advancement of science."

Only before they could advance any science, the body was stolen!

There were a ton of articles about that. The robbery had taken place at 8:07 p.m. on September 26th.

The same date and time as in Dr. F's journal!

I read the rest of the articles. The police never discovered who stole the body. But I knew who had: Dr. Frankenstein. He had taken Bertram III's butt and given it to my dad!

Bertram III was already dead when that happened. But the articles about him also mentioned that he had a son, Bertram IV.

I read online that Bertram IV went to Princeton University, like his dad and granddad and great-granddad. But that was pretty much all I found. I tried to look up a phone number or email for Bertram and came up with nothing.

And the only thing I could find about what he had done after college was that he was now a member of the Princeton Club in New York, USA.

Wait! The Princeton Club of New York! New York! That's where I was!   SWEET!!!

I searched online and found the address of the Princeton Club. It was only a block from the library!

A couple minutes later, I spun through the revolving door of the Princeton Club.

"May I help you?" asked a woman behind the desk in a very quiet voice.

I told her I was looking for Bertram Wodehouse.

"He's in the lounge," she replied as quietly as before. "But I'm afraid our club policy is quite strict. The lounge is a quiet zone."

"Which means," she said in a soft voice, "anything above a whisper will not be tolerated."

She pointed to a table in the back of the lounge. "Bertram is over there," she whispered. "And do keep your voice down."

I saw a man wider than he was tall. He was wearing a jacket and tie and sitting in a very comfy-looking chair having coffee. With Fran Kenstein!!!!

Chapter 13

I didn't know what to do. Should I run? Try to sneak up on Fran and tackle her?

Don't panic, I told myself. *You'll figure something out.* But I didn't get the chance to figure anything out. Because Fran waved me over to their table!

She turned and whispered something to Bertram.

He nodded and waved me over too!

I couldn't just leave my cousin with Fran. So I marched over there.

As Bertram sipped his coffee, Fran ate  some guacamole.

She ate it without chips. Or a spoon. Which didn't look easy. But Fran never did things the easy way.

Whatever Fran was plotting to do to Bertram, she hadn't done it yet. That meant I still had time to warn him.

But I couldn't just tell him we were related through my dad's butt.

What were the odds he'd believe that? And if he didn't believe me, he wouldn't listen to my warnings.

I had to play it smart. I couldn't tell him too much too soon and risk freaking him out.

So I started slow.

"Hi, Bertram," I said. "My name's JD."

"Hello there," replied Bertram as I sat down at his table. "Do I know you? You look a bit . . . peculiar."

I get that a lot — mostly because I've got one green eye and one blue one. And one of my hands is bigger than the other. And one of my legs is shorter than the other.

"JD gets his looks from his dad," Fran said.

"Don't listen to her," I told Bertram. "I mean, yes, I do get my looks from my dad. She's right about that. But she's the reason I'm here to see you. I would've called or emailed, but I couldn't find your number or email address."

"Oh, I don't have email," he replied. "Or a telephone. I thought about getting one once, but buying it seemed like too much trouble. I mean, you have to go to the store. Can you imagine that? Going all the way to a store?!" he said.

That didn't sound like a lot of work to me, but I didn't want to be rude. So I agreed with him.

"I guess when you put it like that, it does sound tough," I said. "It's just that if you had had a phone, it would have been a lot easier to get in touch with you."

"Easier for you, perhaps," he replied with a smile. "But not for me. If I had had a phone, I would have had to pick it up and probably hit some buttons and whatnot to answer it. But since I don't have one, all I had to do is sit here with this nice young woman, while you showed up to tell me whatever it is you want to tell me."

"Well, what I wanted to tell you is that this young woman isn't nice at all!" I exclaimed. "You've got to get out of here, Bertram!"

"SHHH!" hushed several club members.

"Sorry!" I whispered back.

"You shouldn't do that," said Fran.

"What? Talk loudly?" I replied. "Or try to save Bertram?"

"No," she said. "I meant you shouldn't call him Bertram. He prefers Bertie."

"Yes, please call me Bertie," said my cousin. "As I told the young lady, 'Bertram' is such a bother to say."

Chapter 14

"I do not have to believe you," he said. "In fact, it would be far better for me if I did not. Because if I believed what you said, JD, it would ruin this perfectly pleasant coffee I'm having and require me to get up and do something."

"And there's nothing that's more of a bother than doing something," added Bertie. "I've spent my whole life avoiding it."

Fran just sat there smiling.

It began to dawn on me why she hadn't done anything yet. Because she didn't have to. She had all the time in the world.

Bertie didn't seem like he was going anywhere. And since he weighed more than twice as much as me, there was no way I could make him move.

I had to convince him.

"Okay, I know this is a little hard to believe," I told Bertie. "But my dad was Frankenstein's Monster. And he got his, well, rear end from your dad. And I inherited my tush from him. Which means we're related through our butts!"

Bertie shook his head. "I simply refuse to believe it."

"I know it's a little hard to swallow," I admitted. "But it's the truth." I told him about my other cousins and how I had found them through my dad's feet, eye, and guts.

"Oh, no, you misunderstand," said Bertie. "I don't find it preposterous that we are related through our posteriors."

"And I have no trouble at all believing in monsters," he went on. "After all, one of my best friends in the club is one. Isn't that right, Tutty?"

Bertie waved over to the next table.

It was only then that I saw that the person at the next table wasn't a person at all. It was the Mummy!

Man, did that guy stink! I mean, yeah, he smelled bad. He probably hadn't changed his bandages in over 3,000 years. But he also stunk as a person.

A couple years ago, he made a huge mess in my hometown. Some people said it had all been a misunderstanding. Which I guessed made sense — it was impossible to understand his moans and groans. But no one from Victorville would ever be happy to see this guy.

Of course, Bertie wasn't from Victorville. He waved cheerfully at the Mummy.

"UNHHHH!" groaned the Mummy as he waved back at Bertie.

"SHHHHH!" whispered the club members at a nearby table.

I knew they didn't like it when people raised their voices in here. I guessed they didn't like it when mummies did it either.

Bertie turned to me. "So I have no difficulty in believing that it's quite possible my father's rear end could have gone into Frankenstein's Monster. And that that monster is your father."

"Great! Then you know we're related!" I exclaimed.

"SHHH!!!" hushed the people around us.

"I do not believe we are related at all," Bertie whispered to me. "How could I be related to someone like you through my father's posterior? After all, my father sat on that rear end in this very same club I am a member of now, doing nothing for his whole life. Just as my grandfather did. And just like I'm doing now."

Bertie pointed over his shoulder. Hanging on the wall above him were framed paintings of his father and grandfather. They were sitting in the club in the very same chair Bertie was sitting in now.

"For generations," said Bertie, "my family has done nothing. Zero. Bupkis. Zilch. Sorry. I threw in a few foreign words at the end there. Couldn't help it. I was educated at Princeton, after all," he told me. "What I'm saying is: you told me you have raced all around the world chasing after your cousins, correct?"

I nodded. That was true.

"Well, it exhausts me just to think about having such an adventure," said Bertie. "My goal in life is to have no goals in life. Just like my father and his grandfather. You are simply nothing like my family."

"And that," Bertie continued, "means we can't be related. Which means I'm not in any danger from Ms. Kenstein here. Which is wonderful. Because if I were in danger, I'd have to do something about it. And that would interfere with my schedule."

"I always follow the same schedule every day," said Bertie. "After all, trying to think of something new to do every day is an awful lot of work. Sticking to my schedule allows me to avoid all that bother."

"You always do the exact same thing every day?" Fran asked pointedly.

"Absolutely," beamed Bertie, then his face darkened. "Well, except for one day. March eighteenth. Seven years ago. I did something very different that day."

"What?" I asked.

"I skipped my noontime coffee at the club! It was a disaster!" he shuddered. "I will never stray from my schedule like that again!"

He looked at his watch. "In which case, I need to get going," he said.

9AM—
Try AND WAKE UP

10 AM—
Actually WAKE UP

12 PM—
coffee at the Princeton Club

2PM—
Return to room at the St. Regis Hotel to Read the newspaper

4PM—
Tea at the Rainbow Room

6PM—
Dinner at the Club

7PM—
Coffee at the St. Regis Hotel

8PM—
Go to bed

Bertie got up and started to leave.

I looked at Fran.

I expected her to tackle him and grab his butt.

Maybe not grab it. But, well, you know what I mean. But Fran just sat there smiling as Bertie walked away.

Instead of doing anything about his butt, she just sat on hers and said to me, "So, here we are."

Yeah, I thought, *here I am with a crazy person who wants to chop up my cousins to build a new monster! And it's not like she has any nicer plans for me!*

So then why was she just letting Bertie walk away?

"It's not often we find ourselves sitting together in a nice place like this, is it?" she asked.

That was true.

Mostly because every time we met, Fran did things like try to get me arrested or light the air around me on fire with an air fryer!

Wait — was that why she let Bertie go? Because she wanted to take care of me first?

Fran leaned in and whispered, "You've kept me from three of your cousins so far. This time, I am going to stop at nothing to get my hands on Bertie's butt."

"Then why'd you let him go?" I shouted.

"SHH!!" hushed the club patrons.

"I didn't," whispered Fran. "He's with my associate now."

I looked over and saw Bertie getting his coat from the coat check. Then he headed to the door.

"I don't see anyone with him," I whispered back.

"Of course you don't!" gloated Fran, a little too loudly for the other club members.

"SHH!" they all hushed her.

Fran scowled. Then she scribbled something on a napkin and slid it over to me.

Who do you know that you've never seen?

I read Fran's note.

I immediately knew who she had to have meant.

"You mean, my dad!?!" I exclaimed loudly.

"Shh!" said the club patrons again.

"I've never seen him because I never got to meet him!" I whispered at Fran. "Do you know where he is?!"

"Well, actually, I —" started Fran. Then she stopped and said, "That's a story for another time. My note wasn't about your father. Think again. Who is someone you've met that you've never seen?"

"How could I meet someone without seeing them?" I asked. "I mean, they'd have to be invisible or —"

Oh, no!

I knew who Fran meant.

THE INVISIBLE MAN!

"I can see you know who I mean." Fran smiled. "Given what happened the last time you met him, the Invisible Man has given up on getting revenge on the Vampire."

Okay, well, that's good, I thought.

"Now he wants revenge on YOU!" said Fran.

"That's why he's helping me," said Fran. "I figured you'd show up and try to interfere again. I am very smart, after all."

Chapter 15

"So I told the Invisible Man that if he worked for me, he'd be bound to run into you," Fran went on. "All I asked in exchange is that he grab Bertram first. That's why I was happy to sit here, doing nothing. I was waiting for Bertram to get outside where the Invisible Man is waiting to grab him!"

It looked like that was about to happen. Well, okay, it didn't look like that. All I could see was Bertie putting his coat on and walking out through the club's revolving door.

But I knew the Invisible Man had to be somewhere right outside.

There was no way I could run all the way across the club in time. And even if I could, what would I do then? Tackle the Invisible Man? How? I couldn't even see him.

But he could hear me.

"Yo! Invisible Man!" I shouted.

"Shhh!!!" hushed the club members around me.

"I'm right here!" I shouted. "I'm the one you want!"

All the club members looked at me like I was crazy. Including Bertie. And the Mummy, who GROAAAANED.

But it worked! Suddenly, the revolving door to the club spun. Then one table, and then another tipped over and fell to the floor.

The Invisible Man was knocking them over as he made his way to me! Of course, Bertie didn't know that was what was happening. So he turned and walked out onto the street. He was safe!

But I wasn't!

"No!" Fran shouted at the Invisible Man as he ran toward me. "What are you doing? Go back and get Bertram before he gets away!"

"SHH!" a club member shouted back at her.

"Oh, will you be quiet?" said an exasperated Fran.

"Will YOU?" replied the club member.

Fran scowled and turned back to my chair. Which was empty! While she had been distracted by the club member, I had taken off running.

I didn't know if I could make it past the Invisible Man to the front door. So I took off in the opposite direction, hoping there was another way out.

Napkins and glasses flew off tables behind me. The Invisible Man was chasing after me! Which meant he wasn't chasing Bertie. That was good. But if he caught me, that would be bad. Very bad!

I ran through a door and into the kitchen. I ran
past fryers or grillers or whatever you call those
things that cook food.

At the very end of the kitchen, I found a door and
burst through it.

Outside, I found myself on the sidewalk and
stopped to take a deep breath of New York City air.
It smelled like a mixture of garbage and cat pee.

"Oh, this is too gross!" said a voice.

I turned back and saw a piece of gum stretch up
from the sidewalk into the air.

It took me a second, but then I realized the
Invisible Man must have stepped in that gum and now
it was stuck to his foot!

"Ack!" cried the Invisible Man. "Gum on my toes!"

Wait, his toes? Shouldn't the gum be stuck to the bottom of his shoes?

"And **BRRRRR** it's cold out here!" he groaned.

Cold? I guess it was a little chilly. But I felt fine just wearing my T-shirt and jeans.

That's when I realized — Holy crud! Of course! — the Invisible Man wasn't wearing any shoes. Or any clothes at all! GROSS!!!!

I hadn't thought about it before, but it made total sense. His body was invisible, not his clothes. So if I couldn't see him, that meant he was . . . naked. Eww!

I was glad I hadn't realized that when he was chasing me around the Vampire's retirement community! I probably would've been so grossed out that he would have caught me!

But now that I knew, I couldn't let it distract me. I had to focus on escaping him, so I could get back to Bertie before Fran got to him.

As the Invisible Man's invisible hand pulled the gum off his invisible foot, I ran out of the alley — and then stopped short. On to a busy street! A car whizzed by, just missing me.

Nearby, a policeman trotted up on a horse. For a second, I hoped he was coming to help. But he just blew his whistle at me.

"What are you doing running in the middle of the street? Come on, move along!" shouted the policeman. "There's nothing to see here."

"I know," I told him. "That's the problem!"

The Invisible Man could have been anywhere. He could have been in front of me, to the right, or left.

And then suddenly, I felt someone grab my shoulder from behind!

Chapter 16

The hand that had grabbed me spun me around. I saw I was facing an ice cream truck.

"JD, is that you?" said the man hanging out the truck's open back door. "What are you doing in the middle of the street in New York City?"

MR. SHELLEY

It was Mr. Shelley! My old orphanage director!

I didn't waste any time saying hello or asking Mr. Shelley what he was doing here. I dove in the truck, slammed the door behind me, and locked it.

"Hey!" roared the other man in the truck.

I'd never met him, but I recognized the man immediately. He was Mr. Shelley's brother-in-law. He sounded even meaner in person than he did yelling at Mr. Shelley over the phone.

Mr. Shelley introduced me to his brother-in-law as a former orphan from his former orphanage.

"This is the kind of orphan you had at the orphanage?" sneered the brother-in-law as he looked at my mismatched eyes and too-big feet. "No wonder you couldn't make any money in that business!"

"Not that you're any good at making money at this business either!" he added. "Besides being married to your sister, I can't think of one good reason why I shouldn't fire you!"　　　　◀＿＿＿ RUDE!

Mr. Shelley just hung his head.

After leaving the orphanage, Mr. Shelley went to work for his brother-in-law in Las Vegas. He had the idea to drive their ice cream truck to New York.

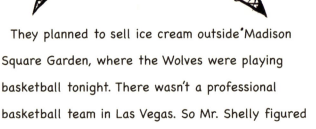

They planned to sell ice cream outside Madison Square Garden, where the Wolves were playing basketball tonight. There wasn't a professional basketball team in Las Vegas. So Mr. Shelly figured they were bound to sell more ice cream in a place that had one.

The problem with Mr. Shelley's idea was that he wasn't the only one who had had it. There were already lots of other ice cream trucks in New York selling ice cream to the fans.

After driving all the way from Las Vegas, Mr. Shelley and his brother-in-law hadn't sold any ice cream at all.

Suddenly, someone pounded on the truck.

I didn't look to see who it was. It wouldn't have helped anyway. It had to be the Invisible Man!

"Finally, a customer!" shouted the brother-in-law.

"No, wait!" I cried. The brother-in-law didn't listen.

He stuck his head out the window.

"Hey, there's no one out here!" he said.

I knew there was someone out there. And it was only a matter of time before he was in here. Unless we got out of there.

"We gotta go!" I cried.

"We're not going anywhere," roared the brother-in-law. "There was a customer out there a second ago. He might come back."

BOOM! BOOM! BOOM! The

Invisible Man pounded on the side of the truck again.

"Ya see?" The brother-in-law beamed as he leaned out the window again. "There he is — Hey! Where'd that customer go?!"

"Right here!" I said.

"What are you talking about?" asked Mr. Shelley.

"I'll be your customer!" I said. "I'll buy all the ice cream you've got! Just get me out of here!"

"Yeah, right," snorted the brother-in-law. "How is an orphan going to pay for $514 worth of ice cream?"

"With this!" I said, holding up a few gold coins. The brother-in-law grabbed one and took a bite. CLANG!

"Tastier than rocky road with colored sprinkles on top!" he cried. "This'll pay for our whole trip — and then some! You're okay, kid!"

Then he gave Mr. Shelley a hug. "And you too, Shelley! You found us our best customer yet!"

"Good old JD!" beamed Mr. Shelley, "You're always there right when I need you!"

Believe me — as we raced away down the street in the ice cream truck, leaving the Invisible Man behind — I said the same thing to Mr. Shelley!

Chapter 17

Ten minutes later, I was standing outside Bertie's hotel room, holding $514 worth of melting ice cream in my arms.

SO STICKY!

I knew where he was because it had been on his schedule. Which meant the Invisible Man and Fran knew too.

I had a head start thanks to the ride Mr. Shelley had given me. There was no way the Invisible Man had gotten here before me. As I pounded on the door, I just hoped Fran was with him — and not already inside with Bertie.

"Oh, it's you," said a very surprised Bertie as he opened the door. "Well, this is unusual."

"Is Fran in there with you?" I asked.

"No," replied Bertie. "I never have visitors at this time. It's not on the schedule. But I do like ice cream. I suppose if I turned you away, I'd have to walk you down to the lobby. You did bring me ice cream, so that would be the only polite thing to do . . ."

He shuddered at the thought. "That's simply too much work," he sighed. "So come on in."

I did. Bertie's hotel room was AMAZING!

It had two bathrooms! And four TVs! Two of which were in the bathrooms! I'd never been in a hotel room with TVs in the bathrooms.

Actually, I had never been in a hotel. The whole thing was pretty cool. But I didn't have time to check it all out.It was only a matter of time before Fran and the I.M. showed up.

I had to get Bertie out of there.

There was just one problem with that: Bertie. He refused to leave his room.

"Go? Oh, I wish you hadn't suggested that," he said as he finished his third ice cream. "Just thinking about it is exhausting. I think I need to lie down."

Bertie flopped down on the bed.

"Ah, yes, much better," he smiled. "I think a good lie down makes most everything better. Don't you?"

I didn't think so at all. In fact, it seemed like the opposite was true: Bertie's lying down was going to make it that much easier for Fran and the Invisible Man to catch up to us. We had to get out of there.

But not before I checked out the TV in the bathroom. Okay, I admit it — that was too cool to pass up. I had never used the bathroom while watching TV, and with Fran and the Invisible Man after me, I didn't think I'd get another chance.

Once that was done, we had to get out of there!

I did everything I could to convince him or cajole him or whatever you call it when you try to get someone to do something. But he wouldn't budge.

I knew it wasn't smart to get annoyed, but I couldn't help it. After all I had done, couldn't he do just a little bit?

"Yes, well, that's you, JD," said Bertie, not even making the effort to lift his head off the pillow to look at me. "Apparently, you enjoy doing things. I don't."

The only thing he wanted to do was the next thing on his schedule: wait to get today's newspaper from the hotel bellboy.

"Of course, I don't actually read the paper," explained Bertie. "That would take too much effort. But I do like to get the paper every day — like my father and my grandfather did."

If I wanted to save Bertie's butt, I had to get him out of there. So, thinking fast, I raced out into the hallway. There was the bellboy, marching toward the door, carrying the newspaper.

"Wait! Stop!" I said. "Please, I'm begging you. You've got to tell him you're out of papers and that he has to go out and get one himself."

"Why would I?" asked the bellboy. "If I do that, I won't get a tip."

That made sense to me. "What if I give you this?" I said, handing him one of the Vampire's gold coins.

"Done!" exclaimed the bellboy, marching into Bertie's room. "We're out of newspapers today, Mr. Wodehouse. "You'll have to go downstairs and get your own." And with that, the bellboy turned and left.

"What a bother!" exclaimed Bertie. "Even if I don't read it, I do like to get the paper every day. It's what my dad and my granddad did. Even more, it's what's on my schedule!"

"You still can," I said. "All we have to do is go downstairs and find a newsstand."

"I don't know," replied Bertie. "That sounds like an awful lot of work."

"Oh, no, it'll be easy," I said.

Luckily, I was wrong. It wasn't easy at all.

We walked for blocks. There were no newsstands anywhere we looked. It turned out, no one bought newspapers anymore. They all got the news on their phones.

Bertie pulled his jacket and scarf closer around him. "It's a bit chilly out here," he complained as his stomach RUMMBLED queasily. "And all this activity definitely does not agree with my digestion. Perhaps we better go back to the hotel."

"No!" I cried. Fran and the Invisible Man had to be at the hotel by now. We couldn't go back there.

"I mean, no," I said in a calmer voice. "Nowadays, everyone gets the news on their phone. That's what we're going to have to do too."

"But I don't have a phone," Bertie reminded me.

"Then let's go buy one!" I replied.

"Buy one?" said Bertie with a look of shock. "How?"

"We find a store," I said as patiently as I could. "And then you take out some money or a credit card and pay for it,"

"Money? A credit card?" he repeated, as if they were foreign words. "I don't have any of those things!"

"You don't?" I said. "Not to be rude, but aren't you pretty rich?"

Bertie thought for a moment. "I think so," he said. "But someone else deals with all that for me. I just put everything on my bill at the club or the hotel."

"Then I'll buy you a phone," I said, dragging Bertie down the street. "I've still got some more gold coins. If you want to keep to your schedule, this is the only way to do it. It'll be easy. I'll take care of everything."

Bertie followed, but he had his doubts. Which he should have.

I didn't know anything about phones. I didn't even have one. That's why I figured it would take us a long time to buy one when we got to the store.

I mean, no one wants to help a kid when you go into a store like that. Everyone's worried you'll break something.

That turned out to be true. Until Bertie mentioned to the salespeople I had a pocket full of gold coins!

After that, I couldn't get them to stop helping me. They even printed out the selfie Bertie took of the two of us with the phone.

Still, everyone in the store was so busy showing Bertie all the things the phone could do, it seemed like we would be there for hours.

Until suddenly — FRRRRRRT!

"Excuse me," said Bertie as he farted again. "My stomach is not used to all this activity."

After that, it took them less than a minute to take my gold coins and hustle us out onto the sidewalk with Bertie's new phone. I couldn't blame them. It smelled like doing stuff REALLY disagreed with Bertie. *PEWWW!*

We stood there on the corner as Bertie played with his new phone. I hoped he would keep doing that all day while Fran and the Invisible Man waited for him back at the hotel.

BEEP! BOOP! Went the phone. BEEP! BEEP! FARRTTT! That last one wasn't the phone. It was Bertie.

I felt bad that making him do stuff was upsetting his stomach. But it was the only way I could think to keep his butt out of Fran's hands. And it seemed to be working. Until a huge car pulled to a stop in front of us. An equally huge driver jumped out and raced right toward Bertie!

"I've come for you," said the driver.

Chapter 18

I leaped between the driver and Bertie.

"Stop!" I cried. "Don't get any closer to him."

But Bertie was already halfway in the car. I tried
to yank him out, but the driver pulled me off him.

"Kid, I'm just trying to do my job here," said
the driver.

"Yeah, right — your job kidnapping people for Fran!"
I said in the bravest voice I could muster. I put up
my dukes or my ducks or whatever you call it when
you raise your fists. "How did you track us down?"

"Look, kid, I didn't 'track you down,'" said the driver, ignoring my dukes or ducks or whatever you call them. "I'm just trying to get a tip here. The hotel manager sent me straight over after Mr. Wodehouse texted him asking for a ride."

"Indeed I did!" said Bertie as he opened the door to the back of the car. "Thanks to this new telephone JD here purchased for me!"

Oh, crud!

I had hoped buying a phone would take so long that Bertie would forget about his schedule. Instead, all the phone did was enable him to text for a ride that would get him right back on schedule!

Wherever he was going to be next, Fran and the Invisible Man were sure to be there waiting for him.

Of course, I tried to tell Bertie that. But Bertie wouldn't listen. "A ride should do wonders for my stomach," continued Bertie. "Not to mention my legs.

I haven't done this much walking around since . . . well, I don't think I've ever done this much walking!"

It felt like my brain was going for a swim inside my head. I didn't know what to do. Until I felt the gold coins in my pocket! I still had a few!

As Bertie settled into the back of the car, I dove into the front.

"How would you like a really big tip?" I whispered to the driver.

"A lot better than a small one," he admitted.

Five minutes later, Bertie and I were back on the sidewalk.

"I can't believe the hotel sent us a limousine that needed an immediate repair," scowled Bertie.

I couldn't believe it either. Because it wasn't true.

I had given the driver three gold coins to lie and say he couldn't get us back to the hotel.

"First the hotel runs out of newspapers, and now this!" said Bertie. "If I didn't find change so exhausting, I might consider moving hotels!"

Bertie looked at his watch. "Speaking of moving," he said. "I have to get to the Rainbow Room for my four p.m. tea!"

Bertie took out his phone to call for another limo.

"NO!" I cried. Then I said in a calmer voice, "You said it yourself. The hotel has already messed up twice today. Can we really risk it?"

"You're right." Bertie nodded. "But what else can we do?" he asked.

I looked around, trying to think of an answer. And saw an entrance to the subway. "We could take the subway," I suggested.

"The subway?" replied Bertie. He had never taken it.

Neither had I. I had no idea how to do it. Probably, it would take a while to figure out.

Which was perfect!

Down in the subway station, Bertie and I looked at the map.

"I attended cartography classes at Princeton," he told me. "That's the study of maps, in case you don't know."

"So what's the map say?" I asked.

"Attending the classes was troublesome enough," Bertie replied. "Actually learning any of it?" He shook his head. "That would have been far too much work."

I had never taken a cartography class, but I did have the blood of an explorer (and also his feet).

I looked at the map. And immediately saw that the Rainbow Room was only one stop away.

I didn't tell Bertie that. Since he couldn't read the map, instead of taking one stop, we'd take ALL the stops.

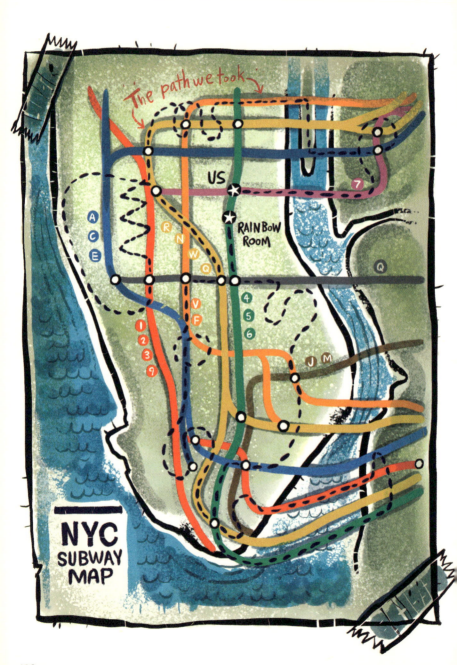

We would have kept riding, but all the activity started to disagree with Bertie and, well, you know . . . FRRRRRTTT! The other passengers made us get off at the next stop.

As we crawled out of the subway station into the setting sun, Bertie looked at his watch. "We're going to be late for the next thing on my schedule," he said.

I was glad to hear it.

"That is we would be," he continued. "If the next place I needed to be weren't right here!"

Needless to say, I wasn't as glad to hear that.

The next thing on Bertie's agenda was tea at the Rainbow Room. Which turned out to be at the top of an incredible New York City skyscraper.

the
RAINBOW
Room

When the elevator let us out on the top floor, a waitress was there to meet us.

"Welcome back, Bertie," she said.

The waitress led us through the restaurant to the balcony. There were several tables there, sixty-five stories above Sixth Avenue. Bertie and I sat at one.

As Bertie read the menu, I realized this wasn't going to be a problem. As soon as he ordered, I would just slip away and then use another gold coin to pay the waitress to say they were out of tea.

And we still had time. Looking at the other tables, I didn't see any sign of Fran. I did see the Mummy at one table (it still bugged me what he had done to my town, but I had bigger worries at the moment). At the other tables were a bunch of really tall men.

And — oh, crud — the Werewolf!

Chapter 19

If there was anyone in the world who hated me more than Fran and the Invisible Man, it was the Werewolf.

My cousin Sam and I had sent him to jail after — well, that's a whole other story (in fact, it's the story right before the last story in my journal, if you don't remember).

The Werewolf was sitting with the tall men in uniforms. Bertie probably weighed the same as one of them, but he was wider than he was tall. We didn't stand a chance.

The Werewolf raised a paw in the air. And asked a waiter, "May we see some menus?"

That's when I noticed that the uniforms the tall men were wearing all said "Wolves."

The "Werewolf" wasn't the Werewolf at all. He was the mascot for the Wolves basketball team. Whew!

Bertie hadn't even noticed I'd been nervous. He'd been busy studying the menu.

I looked over his shoulder and saw that they didn't have any regular food like PB&J or Chicken Fingers. I mean, they kind of did. But it was all a bit different.

I guess that's what made fancy restaurants fancy — they take food you like to eat and then make it kind of strange.

"I don't know why I even bother to look at the menu," Bertie told me. "I always order the same thing: high tea at the highest temperature. In fact, they always bring it to me without having to order."

Okay, all I had to do was give the waitress a gold coin and ask her to tell Bertie the restaurant was out of tea.

I reached into my pocket to pull one out. And came up with nothing but pocket. I was out of coins!

The waitress walked up with the tea. I was doomed.

Even worse, by the time Bertie finished his tea, we'd be finished. Because that would give Fran all the time she needed to get here.

I saw the waitress approach with Bertie's tea.

All I could think was, *This really stinks.* That was partly because I don't like the smell of tea. But it was mostly because now that his tea was coming, Bertie wasn't going anywhere. He was going to stick to his schedule.

After everything I had done today, Bertie was going to sit here until he was done.

I knew there was nothing I could do to change his mind. So I didn't say anything. Bertie didn't say much either. Just two words to the waitress who held his tea: "No thanks."

"But isn't this what you always order?" replied the confused waitress. "Is there something wrong?"

"There's nothing wrong at all!" said Bertie with a smile. "Quite the opposite, in fact! I've had a delightful day doing things for myself. Have you ever tried it? It's really quite interesting!"

The waitress assured Bertie that she'd done many things for herself. Several that very day, in fact.

"Then you know all about it," exclaimed Bertie. "I'm just learning. I had no idea it could be so invigorating. Not great for the stomach," he admitted. "But wonderful for the mind!"

Then Bertie did something even more shocking. He got up! Out of his chair!

"Let's go get our own tea, JD. I'm sure we can find some in a . . ." he paused for a moment. "What do you call those places that sell foodstuffs?" he asked.

"A supermarket?" I replied.

"Yes, that's what I'm talking about!" he exclaimed. "I've been driven past them before. Never been inside. A supermarket. Sounds exciting! Like a place where a superhero would have an adventure!"

I couldn't imagine any hero having an adventure in a grocery store. But that was okay.

I didn't want excitement. I wanted the opposite. Anywhere that wasn't on Bertie's schedule would be safe and quiet. A grocery store was as good a place as any.

I relaxed for the first time in hours.

All my problems were solved! Including the problem of having no more gold coins. Since Bertie turned away his tea without tasting it, we didn't even have to pay for it.

Yup, it definitely looked like my luck was looking up, as I looked over from our table at the elevator.

DING!

The doors slid open. Perfect timing!

One passenger stepped out. Unfortunately, it was Fran.

 OH NUTS!

Chapter 20

As Fran walked through the restaurant, tables flew up in the air behind her.

Of course, I knew it was the Invisible Man knocking them over. But no one else did. They panicked.

Except the Wolf mascot and the Wolves. They got everyone else to the stairs and out of the restaurant.

By the time Fran reached us on the balcony, Bertie and I were all alone.

"Hello there, Fran," he said. "We were just leaving."

"No, you're leaving with me," she replied. "And I doubt JD is leaving here at all."

"Isn't that right?" she said to no one at all.

"Yeah," grunted the Invisible Man.

I heard him rush at me. I was right up against the edge of the balcony. There was nowhere to run. I looked around for something — anything! — I could use to stop him. All I saw was the tea the waitress had brought for Bertie.

The super-high-temperature tea!

As I heard the Invisible Man charge at me, I poured the tea all over the floor. His invisible — and naked! — feet hit the super-hot tea.

It didn't bother me, Bertie, or Fran. Because we were wearing shoes. But it burned the Invisible Man's bare feet!

"Yow!! Ow!! Ow!!" he cried as he jumped around in pain. But the hot tea was everywhere. He leaped up, only to splash down in more hot tea. "Yow!" he cried as he hopped up again — right over the balcony railing!

"Ahhhhhhhhh!" he cried as he fell. I couldn't see if he smashed down to the ground or stopped his fall somehow. He was invisible, after all.

But I had bigger worries. Because as the Invisible Man fell over the railing, he pushed me over too!

I tumbled over the side of the balcony. It reminded me of the time I fell out of the plane over Antarctica. Only I was a lot higher up now.

And instead of soft snow there was nothing but concrete below!

Suddenly, a rope fell down alongside me. I grabbed it. It was slimy. And it smelled like it hadn't been washed in a thousand years.

It hadn't. Because this was no rope. It was the Mummy's bandage!

No matter how bad the Mummy's bandage smelled, I had to admit this guy didn't stink! He was okay in my book. Now I just had to survive long enough to write that down in my book!

The Mummy had unwound most of himself to save me. He couldn't do anything else. Neither could I until I climbed back up.

Bertie was up there with Fran, and there was no one who could help. It was up to Bertie to do something to save himself. Which meant he was doomed.

Fran moved closer to him.

"Bertie," I shouted from below. "Don't just stand there. Do something!"

"'Do something?'" he replied. "You make that sound so easy.

"What should I do? I'm not used to having to come up with things to do!"

"Don't worry," said Fran. "You'll never have to do anything again. You won't be able to escape me this time. Not when I have this!"

She held up her phone.

"It's my brand-new invention," she said proudly. "I call it . . . the Cell Phone!"

"Eh, I don't mean to burst your bubble," said Bertie. "But the cell phone isn't exactly a new invention. I've even got one. Thanks to JD."

He held up his phone.

"That's a cell phone," sneered Fran. "Mine may look like that from the outside, but I've completely rewired it from the inside to turn it into a Cell Phone that will trap you in an impregnable cell!"

Fran powered on her Cell Phone and pushed buttons.

VRRRUM! Her Cell Phone started warming up.

I was hanging a couple dozen yards below them. I couldn't get to Bertie in time. But then I realized that maybe there were other people who could. Police. The Fire Department. Bertie had his phone in his hand. All he had to do was call them!

"Bertie," I cried. "Your phone! Use it!"

"I thought about that," he said. "But it seemed like an awful lot of work and —"

"Do it!!!" I cried.

"Okay," said Bertie.

He held up his phone and . . . threw it at Fran. It wasn't much of a throw. The phone landed about five feet in front of Fran.

"Ah well," sighed Bertie as he slumped down in a comfy chair. "I tried."

"No!" I cried as I climbed up the smelly bandage.

"You didn't! You could still do a lot more!"

"You could," replied Bertie. "Not me. I'm sorry, JD, but I'm just not like you. I think it would just be easier if I let her take me."

"So do I!" agreed Fran as she aimed her Cell Phone at Bertie.

I couldn't believe it. After everything I had done, he wouldn't even get off his butt to save himself. I climbed as fast as I could, but it wasn't fast enough.

All I could do was watch as . . . FRRRRRTTT! Bertie let out the biggest fart yet! Which meant I could do more than watch — I could smell it too!

So could Fran! It was pretty powerful stuff. She stumbled.

And dropped her Cell Phone. Just as it went off! FRZAAAP! A beam of light shot out of it. And hit Fran! She was trapped.

Holy crud! Bertie wouldn't get off his butt to save himself — but then his butt saved him!

The police showed up a little while later, alerted by the Wolves and the rest of the people who had fled the Rainbow Room.

Still trapped by her Cell Phone, Fran was carted away.

Having finally climbed up onto the balcony, I thanked the Mummy. Whatever he had done to my hometown, we were even. And I would make sure everyone back home knew it.

"GRRRRN," replied the Mummy.

Bertie rushed up and gave me a hug.

"We have more in common than I thought!" he exclaimed. "Did you see what I did?"

I had. Well, actually, I had mostly just smelled it. But still. I couldn't have been prouder.

"You did it, Bertie!" I exclaimed. "All by yourself!"

"Well, I did have some help from my posterior," he replied. "But that makes sense. That is how I am related to you, after all."

As the police swarmed around, I whispered to Bertie I had to go. I had learned from past experience that if I got involved with the police, I would have to spend days and days with them. And I couldn't afford to waste that time.

Bertie was safe from Fran for now. But if I knew Fran Kenstein, she would find a way to cause more trouble for my cousins.

I had to find them and warn them first.

As Bertie proudly told the police what he had done ("You'll never believe what I did today," he told them. "I took the subway!"), I tapped my email address into Bertie's phone and then slipped out the back.

About a week later, I got this message:

From: BertramIV@███████████████

Subject: FWD: Letter of Recommendation

Dear JD—Hope you don't mind, but I went ahead and wrote a letter to my alma mater about you. I know you won't be thinking about which college you want to go to for a few years, but when you do, I hope you will consider Princeton. You'd have a very good shot of getting in. You're smart, resourceful, and you're obviously a hard worker. But you've got something that's even more important to have when applying to Princeton: family who went there! It means a lot to the admissions officers, I can assure you. That's what got me in!

Your cousin,
Bertie

Begin forwarded message:
From: BertramIV@███████████████
To: AdmissionsDean@███████████████

Dear Dean,

I'm writing to recommend a young man for admission to Princeton: my cousin, JD. He's got a few years to go, but when he is ready he is exactly the kind of student the University needs. Not only would he learn a lot at Princeton, but everyone would learn a lot from him. I know I did! Like how to ride the subway (Have you ever tried it? It's very interesting!). And even more, he taught me to get off my butt and do things for myself, which — no offense to my former professors — is the most important lesson I have ever learned.

Thank you for your consideration,

Bertram Wodehouse IV

NOT AS SCARY AS HE LOOKS!

Scott Sonneborn has written dozens of books, one circus (for Ringling Bros. and Barnum & Bailey), and a bunch of TV shows. He's been nominated for one Emmy and spent three very cool years working at DC Comics. He lives in Los Angeles with his wife and their two sons.

COOLEST ILLUSTRATOR EVER!

Timothy Banks is an award-winning illustrator known for his ability to create magically quirky illustrations for kids and adults. He has a Master of Fine Arts degree in Illustration from the Savannah College of Art & Design, and he also teaches fledgling art students in his spare time. Timothy lives in Charleston, SC, with his wonderful wife, two beautiful daughters, and two crazy pugs.

I, J.D., dedicate this journal to my dad,
FRANKENSTEIN'S MONSTER.

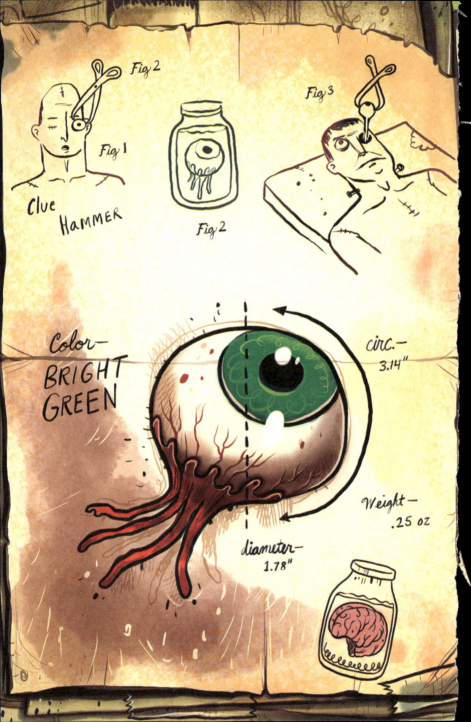